i'm still here

OLGA NEGRIN

D1127736

Copyright © 2021 Olga Negrin.

All rights reserved. No part of this book may be used or reproduced by any means, graphic, electronic, or mechanical, including photocopying, recording, taping or by any information storage retrieval system without the written permission of the author except in the case of brief quotations embodied in critical articles and reviews.

Archway Publishing books may be ordered through booksellers or by contacting:

Archway Publishing
1663 Liberty Drive
Bloomington, IN 47403
www.archwaypublishing.com
844-669-3957

Because of the dynamic nature of the Internet, any web addresses or links contained in this book may have changed since publication and may no longer be valid. The views expressed in this work are solely those of the author and do not necessarily reflect the views of the publisher, and the publisher hereby disclaims any responsibility for them.

Any people depicted in stock imagery provided by Getty Images are models, and such images are being used for illustrative purposes only.
Certain stock imagery © Getty Images.

Interior Image Credit: Olga Negrin

ISBN: 978-1-4808-9988-9 (sc)
ISBN: 978-1-4808-9989-6 (hc)
ISBN: 978-1-4808-9987-2 (e)

Print information available on the last page.

Archway Publishing rev. date: 01/13/2021

dedication page

For Leo. *Love the world as much as I love you.*

When you close your eyes to fall asleep
And open them for one last peep.

Don't worry, I'm still here,
moms never disappear.

When you wake up at three in the morning with very little reason or warning.

Even with a lack of sleep, my love for you always runs deep. No need to cry, I'm still here. Moms never disappear.

When you're having a bad day and you want to run and hide, remember you always have the strength inside.

But just in case you need some cheer, don't worry, I'm still here. Moms never disappear.

When you start making friends besides Mommy, maybe you'll play with Mateo, Grace or Tommy. Just remember: always be sweet to all the kids you meet!

Even if I'm not on the playground, know that I will always be around. In your heart, I'm still here. Moms never disappear.

When you grow up and start to date,
remember to lead with love, never hate.
But if they're mean or not "the one",
don't ever think that love is done.

Straight, gay or queer, don't fear- I'm still here! Moms never disappear.

When everything feels like it's going wrong, know that you're right where you belong.

If people pick on you and make you feel small, remember who you are and stand up tall. Even if I'm not near- I'm still here! Moms never disappear.

When I am old and gray, there will come a day when my body goes away.

Remember that I'm in your heart,
even if we are worlds apart.

Continue to put love out there, even if life seems unfair. The world needs your love and light, spread some hope with all your might!

When you think you need me more than ever, your strength and courage falters never. Take a deep breath and feel me near. Remember my darling, I'm still here.

about the author

Olga Negrin is an art teacher from New Jersey who has worked with children for many years. As a new mom, Olga wanted to create a book that captured the love she has for her own kids.

CPSIA information can be obtained
at www.ICGtesting.com
Printed in the USA
BVHW021158240121
598598BV00028B/2435

9 781480 899889